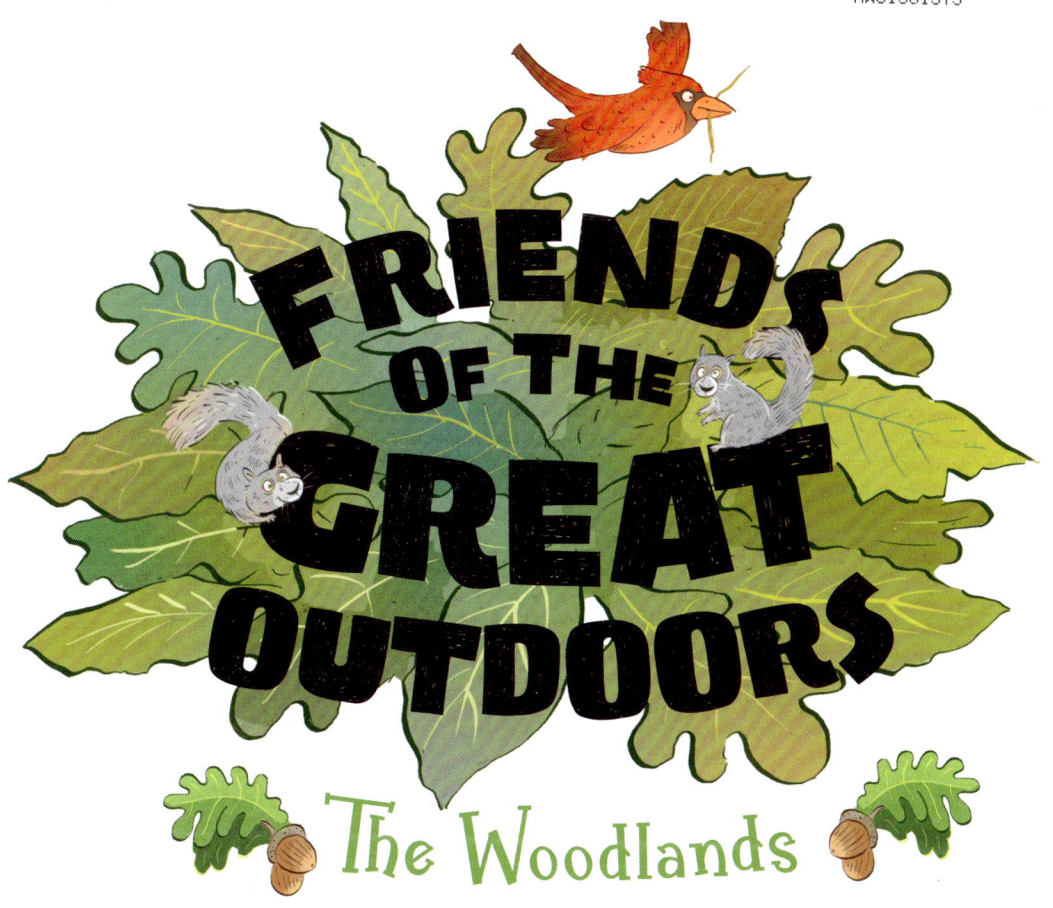

Friends of the Great Outdoors
The Woodlands

By **Hank Thornhill**

Illustrated by **Stephen Stone**

"Once upon a time," Pop-Pop began, "we were friends of

THE GREAT OUTDOORS.

We slept outside. We ate outside. We told stories outside . . ."

"But along the way, we've become friends with

THE GREAT INDOORS.

Now, we play inside. We learn inside. We tell stories inside. We've lost touch with our friend, the great outdoors."

"So what?" Monty said. "I love the indoors! That's where the video games are."

"And the refrigerator!" George added.

Pop-Pop nodded. "It *is* cozy indoors. But all the best adventures are *outdoors.*"

"Adventures? Really?" Rui asked, feeling unsure.

"It's just trees and dirt outdoors. What's so special about that?"

"Just trees and dirt?" began Pop-Pop.

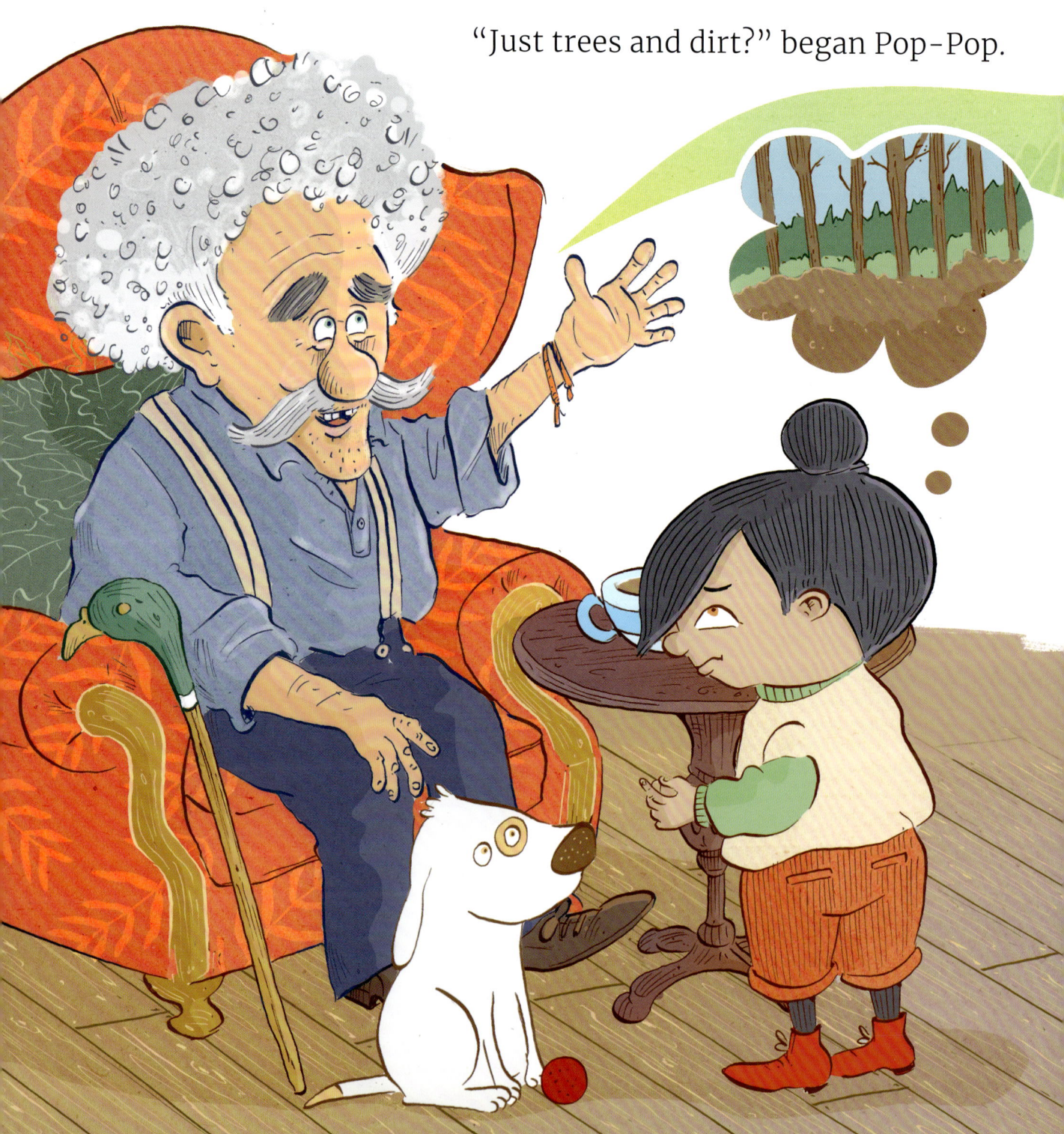

At the word *explore*, Monty, George, and Rui gathered around Pop-Pop.

"I know just the thing for you three," Pop-Pop proclaimed. "A quest . . . if you're willing to take it on. I want you to find **the treasure of the woodland collector!**"

"**The woodland collector?**" Rui echoed.

"That does sound like an adventure!" Monty roared, racing to the back door. "Come on!"

"Wait, guys," George called. "Let's collect a snack first."

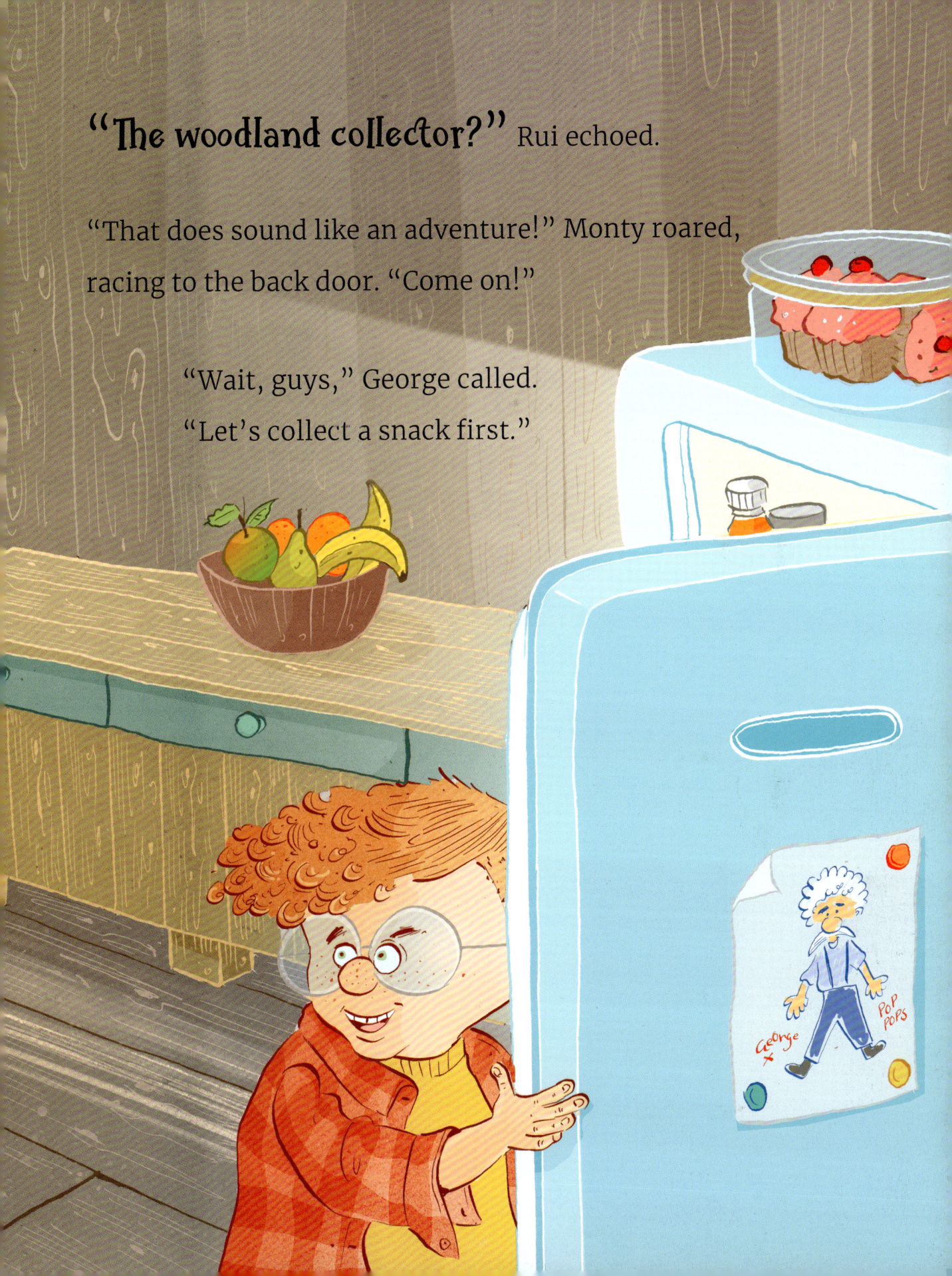

"Hey, look! I found something!" George exclaimed a few minutes later.

Rui elbowed him playfully. "That's a collection, alright! A collection of deer poop!"

"Yeah, but look. Tracks!" Monty pointed out. "Let's follow them. And keep your eyes peeled. The deer are probably still around."

"I don't know about deer," George said, "but I do hear something. Listen to all the birds."

"This one's collecting something. That must be what we're looking for," Monty said, peering through her binoculars.

George shook his head. "I think it's building a nest."

"Birds must be builders then, not collectors," Rui called out wisely. "The search continues. Let's keep loo—**OOHHH,** up there!"

"An owl!" Monty sang.

"It didn't even make a sound!" George said in amazement.

"Let's follow it!"

The three pursued the owl deeper and deeper into the woods.

"Hey, look at this **HUGE** tree!" Rui exclaimed.

"It's laying on the ground."

Monty shivered.

"**EWW,** it's covered in mushrooms. **GROSS!**"

Monty remembered what Pop-Pop had told her.

"Mushrooms keep the forest clean. They eat dead trees and branches that fall on the ground."

"So they're cleaners, not collectors," George pointed out.

"Let's keep exploring!"

PFFT PFFT QUEEE!

"What was that?" Monty asked, reaching for her binoculars.

Rui pointed to a branch over them.

"It's just a squirrel."

PFFT PFFT QUEEE!

"Look, she's got something in her mouth," Monty said. "It's probably just an acorn. Haven't you ever seen a squirrel before? Come on. We should head back."

"Wait," Monty interrupted Rui. "It went into that hole in the log."

"I thought squirrels liked tall trees," George said.

"I wonder what it's doing in a rotten log."

The friends studied the log like scientists in a lab.

A minute went by. Then two.

Suddenly, the squirrel darted out. "Hey, she doesn't have the acorn anymore," Monty said. "Does that mean . . . ?"

". . . that she ate it?" George asked as his stomach growled.

Monty peered into the log.

"She hasn't eaten it yet!" she shouted. "Look!"

Waving her friends over, Monty stepped aside.

"I present to you all:

the treasure of the woodland collector!"

George peered in before looking blankly at his friends.

"The treasure is acorns?"

"Of course! Squirrels collect acorns to eat over the winter."

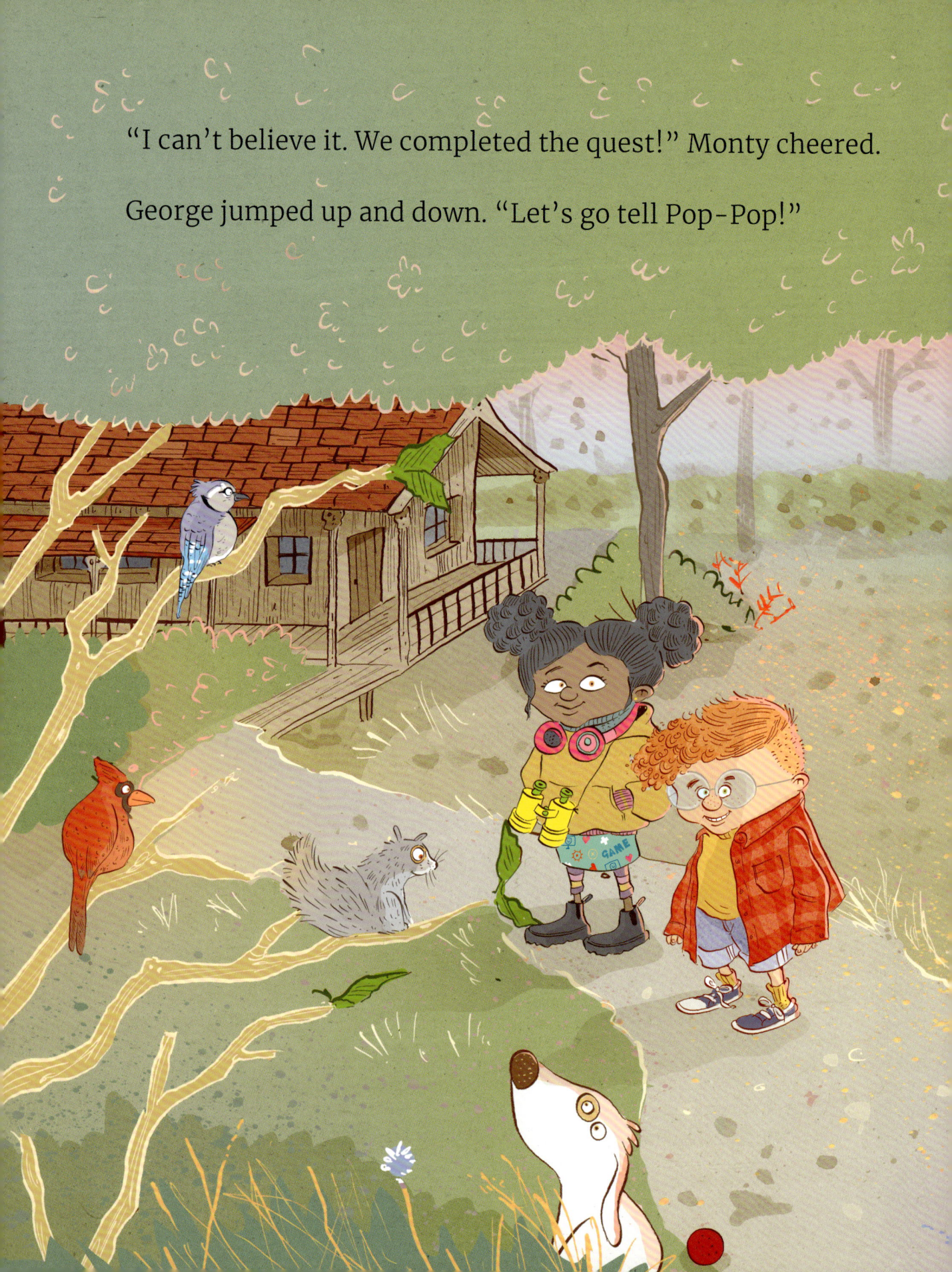

"I can't believe it. We completed the quest!" Monty cheered.

George jumped up and down. "Let's go tell Pop-Pop!"

But Rui wasn't so sure. "Why don't we stay out here? We can use the sticks to make a fort and eat acorns like squirrels. Your Pop-Pop was right, George. It's **GREAT OUTDOORS!**"

Monty put her arm around Rui. "You bet it is. But I have a better idea. How about we head inside and figure out our next great adventure? We can explore all the animals and habitats we want!"

"You mean like the jungle?" Rui asked.

"The jungle! The Arctic! The high desert!
We're going to explore them all because we're the . . .

FRIENDS OF THE GREAT OUTDOORS"

"You guys, that sounds awesome and all," George said, "but first, can we go explore the kitchen?"

FRIENDS OF THE GREAT OUTDOORS
What can you see, hear, feel, and smell in the woods?

Look closely at the ground. The floor of the forest is home to countless itty bitty critters. How many of them can you find?

HERE'S A TIP
A magnifying glass can make small things seem near.

Be still. **Listen.** How many different critters can you hear? Do you hear any birds that sound like an alarm? Sometimes blue jays and crows will alert others when a hawk or owl is near.

In the fall, if you listen closely, can you hear the leaves falling to the ground. What sound do they make?

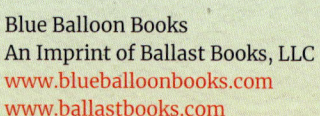

Blue Balloon Books
An Imprint of Ballast Books, LLC
www.blueballoonbooks.com
www.ballastbooks.com

Text copyright © 2024 by Hank Thornhill
www.hankthornhill.com
Illustrations copyright © 2024 Stephen Stone
www.yellowstonestudio.co.uk
Book Design by Stephen Stone

All rights reserved. No part of this book may be reproduced in any form or by any electronic or mechanical means, including information storage and retrieval systems, without permission in writing from the publisher, except by reviewers, who may quote brief passages in a review.

ISBN: 978-1-962202-58-9 (hbk)
ISBN: 978-1-962202-41-1 (pbk)
ISBN: 978-1-962202-44-2 (ebk)

Printed in Hong Kong

Published by Blue Balloon Books
www.blueballoonbooks.com

Blue Balloon Books is always looking for new authors. If you have a book idea, please email: info@blueballoonbooks.com